FOR THE FRIENDS WHO KNEW OF BUMBLE
BEFORE THE BOOK

BUMBLE
THE BEE

WRITTEN AND ILLUSTRATED BY
WILPO MILLOW

Bumble is a hard-working honey bee – a **forager** bee, in fact.

Bumble flies around to find sweet **pollen** and **nectar** for a snack.

Bumble can **fly**!
With her wings, she can **fly**.
High in the sky,
with a **pollen basket** by her side.

She can smell very well!
When she can smell something sweet,
she will know, she can tell,
that it will be a treat.

Sometimes Bumble flies near,
where the **oak trees** are.

Maybe she will visit the **pond**,
but that's rather far.

Today was sunny,
and Bumble loves the Sun.
So she wanted to **adventure**,
she wanted some fun.

She flew past the oak tree and past the pond,
she flew and flew while singing her song.

"I am Bumble. Bumble the bee!
A forager bee. Yes, that's me!"

She found a farm with a small patch of tulips.
Suddenly, the sky was lit with lightning rips.

Storm clouds grew and
then came the wind.

"Oh beeswax!"
exclaimed Bumble,
"what a **pickle** I'm in!"

"Are you lost?" asked a lamb,
passing by back to his **shelter**.
Bumble looked up,
wondering if he would help her.

"Let me take you to my barn,
it will be dry inside."
"Hop on my back,
I'll take you for a ride."

"Oh, thank you so much,"
thanked Bumble as she –
buried herself into the lamb's **fleece**,
"it's so warm and such a relief."

Bumble took a nap
upon the lamb's soft **wool**.

Bzz
Bzz

She needed the rest and
now her **energy** is full!

"What is your name?"
asked Bumble to the lamb,
"I'm Bumble!
Bumble the forager bee, I am!"

"My name is Bleaty,
but you can call me Bleat,
that's what my friends call me
and I'm glad we could meet!"

The rain lightened,
which meant Bumble should go.

So she picked up her basket,
and then let the lamb know.

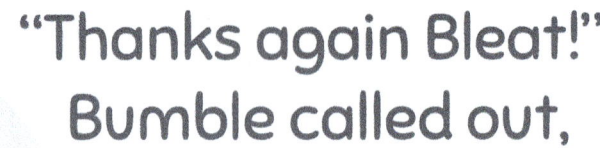

"Thanks again Bleat!"
Bumble called out,

"I will come find you
next time I'm about!"

The rain, although light, still **weighed** down on Bumble's wings.

Tired from flying, she stopped by the pond for a drink.

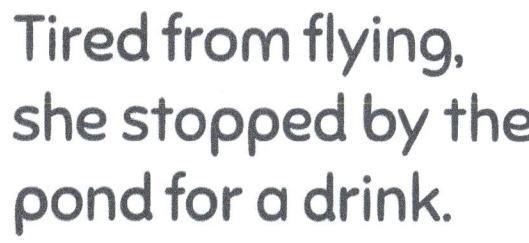

"Oh beeswax!" exclaimed Bumble, "I just want to go home!"

But this rain won't stop and I'm out here all alone!"

"Are you alright?"
chimed a frog who was dancing in the rain,
"you look awfully wet and
I heard you complain."

"I just want to fly back,
but my wings are **soaked**."
"That's no good!"
the pond frog croaked.

The frog leaped
and hopped,
"what a day,
you must have had!"

Then the frog
plucked and pulled
out a small lily pad.

"Take this here,
it will keep you dry.
Keep it over your head,
while you fly!"

"Thank you, kind frog.
Thank you ever so much.
I must be going now,
I'm in quite a **rush**!"

"But before I go,
I just must know –
What is your name?
Thank you for helping me so."

"I'm glad we met,
I'm glad we did!
My name is
Ribbit
but you can
call me Bit."

"That's what my buddies call me.
Find me to play next time you're free!"

"I'm Bumble the bee,
a forager bee.
Next time I'm here –

Definitely!"

Bumble hung the lily pad
above her head,
and began to soar off again,
with her wings out spread.

Suddenly the wind blew,
it was a mighty gust.
So strong that
Bumble's lily pad was thrust.

"Oh beeswax!"
exclaimed Bumble,
"not my lily pad!"

"Today's weather
sure is bad!"

"Are you okay?"
came a squeak through the leaves.
Something was **scurrying**
through the oak trees.

"I am trying to get home
but the wind is too **blustery**,
I want to go home –
I'm in quite the hurry!"

A squirrel popped its head
over and saw Bumble in a mess,
"Why don't you stay over?
It's safer in my nest."

Bumble was welcomed
into the **abode**,
"Thank you for having me
in your lovely home."

"You're welcome,"
pipped the squirrel,
shaking off the rain,
"stay here for a while,
until the wind calms down again."

"What is your name?" asked Bumble politely,
"I want to thank you for being so friendly!"

"My name is Nibbles, but you can call me Bill.
Making new friends is always a thrill!"

"I'm Bumble the bee.
A forager bee.
I am happy we are friends now,
it fills me with **glee**!"

The wind went from
a howl to a whistle.
"Thank you for your help!
Thank you so much, Bill!"

Then off Bumble flew,
no more wind or rain.
Now Bumble can fly
all the way home again.

Bumble bravely brought back
the pollen to the hive.
What a day, what an **adventurous** ride!

Bumble is humbled
and **heartfeltly** thankful,

to have made
so many friends
and it was all so **eventful**.

To Bumble's new buddies,
Bleat, Bit and Bill,
Bumble **believes** that she'll be back,
Bumble believes she will!

Bumble the bee,
was thankful you see.
She was thankful for having
the **courage** to speak.

The words she said,
that we should commend –

was when Bumble said,
"Let's **BEE** friends!"

www.ingramcontent.com/pod-product-compliance
Lightning Source LLC
Chambersburg PA
CBHW082056090726
47909CB00010B/3052